MAE'S FIRST DAY OF SCHOOL

WORDS AND PICTURES BY

KATE BERUBE

ABRAMS BOOKS FOR YOUNG READERS
NEW YORK

THE ILLUSTRATIONS IN THIS BOOK WERE CREATED
WITH INK, FLASHE PAINT, ACRYLIC PAINT, AND
COLORED PENCILS ON COLD PRESS WATERCOLOR PAPER.

Cataloging-in-Publication Data has been applied for and may be obtained
from the Library of Congress.

ISBN 978-1-4197-2325-4

Text and illustrations copyright © 2018 Kate Berube
Book design by Chad W. Beckerman

Printed and bound in China
10 9 8 7 6 5 4 3 2 1

Abrams Books for Young Readers are available at special discounts when
purchased in quantity for premiums and promotions as well as fundraising
or educational use. Special editions can also be created to specification. For
details, contact specialsales@abramsbooks.com or the address below.

ABRAMS The Art of Books
195 Broadway, New York, NY 10007
abramsbooks.com

FOR GIGI

Today is Mae's first day of school.
When her mother said,
"It's time to get dressed!"

Mae said, "I'm not going."

When her father said,
"Eat your breakfast."

Mae said, "I'm not going!"

And when her mother said, "Put on your coat."

Mae said,

"I'M.
NOT.
GOING."

"Now, Mae, that's enough!" said her mother.

On the walk to school, her mother told her all about the fun things she would find there. Things like class pets and great big libraries and long, wild recesses.

On the walk to school, Mae thought about all the things that could go wrong.

Things like, what if the
other kids didn't like her,
and what if she was the only
one who didn't know how
to write, and what if she
missed her mother?

When they got to school, there were lots of other parents and kids outside.

Mae's mother said, "Hello! How are you? Today is Mae's very first day of school, and what a beautiful day it is!"

"Well, isn't that wonderful!" said a man.

"But where is Mae?"
"Mae?" called her mother. "Where are you?"

And Mae answered,
"I'm not going!"

Mae wondered if she could live in this tree.
She thought maybe she could. There was a
mossy spot she could sleep on, and she had
a whole lunch box full of food to eat.

Then Mae heard some rustling.

"Hello," said the small girl.
"Hello," said Mae.

"Rosie! Come down from
that tree right now. School
is starting soon!" called the
man from down below.

"I'm not going to school," said Rosie.

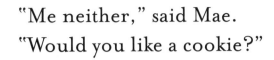

"Me neither," said Mae.
"Would you like a cookie?"

Today is Mae and Rosie's first day of school, but they are not going.

"Why aren't you going to school?" asked Mae.

"Well," said Rosie, "I'm not going because what if no one will play with me?

Or what if I have to read—I don't know how!

Or what if I miss my dad?"

Just then they heard the rustling sound of someone else coming up.

"Hello!" said the tall lady.
"Hello," said Mae quietly.
"We're not going to school."

"That's good," said the tall lady. "I'm not going to school either." And she settled comfortably into a spot on the bottom branch and gazed out through the leaves.

"Who are *you*?"
asked Rosie.

"I'm Ms. Pearl,"
said the tall lady.

"Would you like a cookie,
Ms. Pearl?" asked Mae.
"Yes, please," said Ms. Pearl.

Today is Mae and Rosie and
Ms. Pearl's first day of school,
but they are not going.

"Ms. Pearl, why aren't *you* going to school?" asked Mae.

"Well," she answered, "I'm not going because what if the kids don't like me?

Or what if I forget how to spell Tuesday?

Or what if I miss my cat?"

Mae smiled at Ms. Pearl and Rosie. "You know what? We're all afraid of the same things. I'm glad I'm not the only one."

"Me, too," said Rosie. "And you know what else? You don't have to be worried about nobody liking you because I like you both."

"Me, too," said Ms. Pearl. "And you don't have to be worried about making mistakes when you're reading and writing. School is for learning new things."

"And if we lived
in this tree, we'd
miss our families
anyway," said Mae.

"Plus, we're out of
cookies," said Rosie.

A few minutes later Mae's mother called up,
"School is about to start!"

And Mae said,

"Okay.
Here.
We.
Come!"

Today is Mae and Rosie and Ms. Pearl's
first day of school, and there they go.